This Little Tiger book belongs to:

_____

_____

_____

For mucky kids, everywhere ~ P B

For Alan, with love ~ H G

LITTLE TIGER PRESS
An imprint of Magi Publications
1 The Coda Centre, 189 Munster Road,
London SW6 6AW
www.littletigerpress.com

First published in Great Britain 2011
This edition published 2011
Text copyright © Paul Bright 2011
Illustrations copyright © Hannah George 2011
Paul Bright and Hannah George have asserted their rights to be identified as
the author and illustrator of this work under the Copyright, Designs and Patents Act, 1988
A CIP catalogue record for this book is available from the British Library
All rights reserved • ISBN 978-1-84895-238-6
Printed in China • LTP/1400/0202/0411
2 4 6 8 10 9 7 5 3 1

Boris's Big Bogey

Paul Bright   Hannah George

LITTLE TIGER PRESS
London

When Boris sailed the seven seas
    on the pirate ship Black Rose,
In sun or storm, he always kept
    one finger up his nose.
Yes, even as he scrubbed the decks,
    or trimmed the captain's hair,
He still picked great big bogeys out,
    and flicked them in the air.

Captain Shiver-Me-Timbers,
he let out a sudden cry:
"Look here upon this chart, m'lads.
Do you see what I spy?"

"A far-off treasure island,
what's not been seen afore.
We'll go and search for pirates' gold
upon its distant shore."

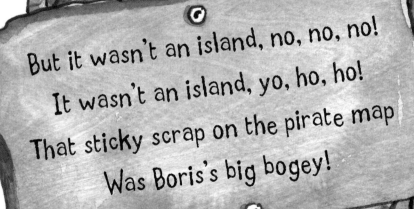

But it wasn't an island, no, no, no!
It wasn't an island, yo, ho, ho!
That sticky scrap on the pirate map
Was Boris's big bogey!

But magic things can happen at sea,
   where storm winds rage and roar.
They sailed and sailed for many a day
   until, at last, they saw
A strange, uncharted island,
   with cliffs all grim and grey.
So they came to Bogey Island,
   and they moored in Bogey Bay.

Then Captain Shiver-Me-Timbers
stood upon the swaying bridge,
And with his big, brass spying glass,
he scanned each rock and ridge.

"I see a cave, all dank and dark,
above the foaming tide.
A pirate's cavern, that's for sure,
with treasure deep inside."

But it wasn't a cave, oh no, no, no!
It wasn't a cavern, yo, ho, ho!
But a glob of goo, in his telescope view,
From Boris's big bogey!

But wondrous things can happen at sea,
  for when they rowed ashore,
They found a cave, a secret cave,
  with a stone across the door,

And a faded sign, which read:
'Keep Out', and 'Here be Pirate Gold!'
So in they went, for pirates
never do what they are told.

KEEP OUT

Here be
Pirate Gold!

Then Captain Shiver-Me-Timbers
held his pirate lantern high,
And in the flickering candlelight
he said, "Oh me! Oh my!"

"I see a chest, a pirates' chest,
part buried in the sand.
We'll dig it up and soon we'll be
the richest in the land!"

But it was not treasure, no, no, no!
Not a chest or casket, yo, ho, ho!
Just a shadow cast
through the lantern glass
From Boris's big bogey!

But strange, strange things can happen at sea,
for when they searched some more,
They found a chest, a pirates' chest,
with gold and coins galore.

They filled their boots, they filled their hats,
they filled their pockets too.
They snatched, they grabbed, they didn't share —
that's not what pirates do!

So, filled with silver and with gold,
the pirate ship set sail.

Then Captain Shiver-Me-Timbers gasped,
and his pirate face grew pale.
"I see a hole, a leaking hole,
below the waterline!
We're doomed and done for!
Sure to sink beneath the salty brine!"

How the crew laughed, ho, ho, ho!
As they told him, "No, no, no!
That blob of black, it's not a crack,
It's Boris's big bogey!"

But they were wrong! It was a hole,
  in the broken, oaken floor.
The sea came 'Splash!' through the gaping gash,
  then more and more and more!

"We need some glue, some gunk or goo,
or else we'll all be drowned!"
So Boris dug deep in his nose,
to see what could be found.

But dreadful things can happen at sea,
for bogeys — there were none!
His nose was clean as a washing machine.
He'd picked and flicked each one.

So Captain Shiver-Me-Timbers cried,
as the water flooded in:
"All pirates, pick your noses!
After one, two, three … begin!"

The pirates prodded,
picked and poked,
to try to stop the leak.

The pirate cats and rats joined in —
the parrot picked his beak.

They picked 100 bogeys,
and they used them,
every one,

All squished and squashed to fill the hole,
until the job was done.

Now all the pirate crew,
    they are as rich as rich can be,
And Boris has a castle tall,
    at Pirateville-On-Sea.

With servants to prepare his tea,
and wash and dry his clothes,
And, yes, there's even one
to stick a finger up his nose!

And the pirates all shout, "Yo, ho, ho!
No more to sea we'll go, go, go!
Hurrah for those who pick their nose,
And Boris's big bogey!"

More Little Tiger adventures to enjoy in sun or storm!

For information regarding any of the above titles or
for our catalogue, please contact us:
Little Tiger Press, 1 The Coda Centre,
189 Munster Road, London SW6 6AW
Tel: 020 7385 6333 • Fax: 020 7385 7333
E-mail: info@littletiger.co.uk • www.littletigerpress.com

For the little, and the big.

A Lothian Children's Book
First published in Australia and New Zealand in 2013
by Hachette Australia
Level 17, 207 Kent Street, Sydney NSW 2000
www.hachettechildrens.com.au
www.shauntan.net

This edition published in 2016

3 5 7 9 10 8 6 4 2

Text and illustrations copyright © Shaun Tan 2013

National Library of Australia
Cataloguing-in-Publication data:

Tan, Shaun, author.

Rules of summer / Shaun Tan.

978 0 7344 1711 4

A823.3

Designed by Shaun Tan
Art photography by Matthew Stanton
Colour reproduction by Hell Colour Australia and Splitting Image
Printed in China by Toppan Leefung Printing Limited

Many thanks to Helen Chamberlin, Tegan Morrison, Jon Appleton, Suzanne O'Sullivan
and the Hachette team, Sophie Byrne, Inari Kiuru, Will Lauria, Julia Adams, Melbourne
Artists' Supplies, Australian Society of Authors, Klaus Humann and Arthur Levine.

A RULES OF SUMMER
APP IS ALSO AVAILABLE
WeAreWheelbarrow.com